Mr

Mr Davies

C.E Okwera

Profyle Publishing

First published in the United Kingdom in 2020 by
Profyle Publishing

All rights reserved
The characters and events portrayed in this book are fictitious. Any similarity to real persons, living or dead, is coincidental and not intended by the author.

Copyright © C.E Okwera 2019
The moral right of the author has been asserted

This book is sold subject to the condition that it shall not, by way of trade or otherwise, be lent, resold, hired out, or otherwise circulated without the publisher's prior consent in any form of binding or cover than that in which is it published and without a similar condition including this condition being imposed on the subsequent purchaser

Profyle Publishing
Suite 214 Tudorleaf Business Centre
London, N15 4QL
www.profylegroup.com

For Manisha Matharu and Florence Israel

CHAPTERS

ONE: Mr Davies

TWO: The Rottweiler

THREE: Mrs Davies

FOUR: P-Squared

FIVE: Perfect Wasn't Enough

SIX: March 28th

SEVEN: The Business Trip

EIGHT: April 02nd

NINE: The Bullet Trick

TEN: Noted

CHAPTER ONE

Mr Davies

Patrick Davies was the Owner and Founder of Pacific Rose. A multimedia company that had mastered the art of evolving with the digital age. A company that he had built from scratch with the help of his wife Pamela in August 2011. The Pacific

Rose brand was held in great esteem and received many business awards and financial rewards. Patrick became very influential in his circle through the success of his company and as his influential power grew so did his arrogance.

    The man had great audacity and strutted into any room with his back upright and chest puffed. He was a handsome man with prominent cheekbones, thin almond eyes, and full lips surrounded by a full beard, bushy and glistening. His shirts were always immaculately pressed and trousers perfectly fitted, slightly hugging his derrière and hemmed with a half break allowing for the shine of his shoes to reflect the light. His suit jackets were also fitted and showcased his biceps. They were single-breasted with two buttons, the lower button worn loosened. The Patrick Davies look was always completed with a tie and Creed or Dior cologne.

Patrick's obsession with his grooming and style stemmed from his father. Mr Davies senior was the most stylish man Patrick knew. He had driven a fire engine red convertible and always had a beautiful woman in tow. He was a music manager for a hip hop artist and toured the world. When Patrick was younger he was taken on tours but when he became of school age it was decided that it would be better for him to stay with his grandmother, where his studies would not be disrupted. Each time Mr Davies senior came to see his son, he would bring the latest trainers and designer outfits.

At the age of fourteen, Patrick had the only mobile phone in school which he charged his schoolmates to use. He attracted attention from girls much older than him and he didn't know how to manage it. The older girls would manipulate him to sell his things and spend money on them. The times when his father had not managed to return home in several months, he noticed that the female attention would dwindle. The girls didn't yearn for his time as he yearned for theirs, they didn't care for him as he cared for them, this hurt young Patrick. But female attention was like a drug, the comedown was depressing, the highs were exhilarating. It boosted his energy, his standing amongst the other boys, and his ego. He now understood why his dad always kept a female in tow. The Davies men thrived off style, money, and confusing ego with self-confidence.

The ego of Patrick Davies worked very well for him in business but in his personal life, it was a burden that constantly required stroking. Mrs Davies did as best as she could but, who has time to constantly feed a grown man's ego when there's shopping to be done, soirées to arrange and lunches to attend. And so Patrick would change executive assistants frequently. Always female, always beautiful, always with toned bodies that fit perfectly into pencil skirts.

CHAPTER TWO

The Rottweiler

The current executive assistant to Mr Davies was Ella Fountayne. Ella was bright, calm, inquisitive, and loyal. She quickly went from pre-meeting clients on behalf of Mr Davies to attending all executive meetings with Mr Davies including those that involved business travel in private jets and staying at the Four Seasons, The Marriott, The Hyatt or The Radisson. No previous "executive assistant" had had such a privilege. Not many in the Pacific Rose headquarters had had such a privilege.

Ella's wit, charisma, and intelligence had completely won over her strong, stern, bully of a boss. Her unbowed loyalty to the boss earned her the alias amongst her senior colleagues of "his Rottweiler". She was well aware of the nickname. She understood the senior management having bitter indignation at not being treated as well as she was. But she paid no concern to it. To be fair, of all the breeds they could have chosen, Rottweiler worked very well as Ella was tall and tanned and forceful. She wouldn't have taken too kindly to "his Poodle".

A poodle is too fluffy, too cute, she is neither. Ella is fearless, alert, and stoic. Her diamond face shape is adorned with soft arch eyebrows, brown almond eyes, and full lips. Her skin is flawless with a small beauty spot on her right cheekbone. Her hair is dark brown and wavy, always tied back into a neat bun with a sharp middle part. If she wore makeup it was very subtle, she would powder her t-zone before meetings and reapply lip gloss.

Her office set was always simple, a satin shirt paired with a pencil skirt, tights and Louboutin heels. Heels which she strutted firmly around the office in, with access to all areas. Her raspy voice could be heard chairing meetings in board rooms but also in reception having a gossip with Vincenzo, who was gay in character and sexuality. Vincenzo left Ella to strut while he flounced, he enjoyed every part of being the work bestie of the Rottweiler, and the Rottweiler, in turn, indulged in his freeness to divulge office secrets and rumours.

CHAPTER THREE

Mrs Davies

Mrs Davies was well aware of the ever-changing executive assistants at Pacific Rose headquarters and was kept up-to-date on all office goings-on by the perennial gay bestie, Vincenzo.

Pamela Davies née Kimara had met Patrick at a networking event that her friend Hannah had organised. As Pamela was handing out business cards and explaining the services offered at her PR agency, the athletic silhouette of Patrick entered the room and headed for the bar. He ordered a Hennessy on the rocks, took a sip, and turned to survey the room. His entrance had irked Pamela. The audacity of this man, she thought. He arrived late, didn't apologize to the host, headed straight to the bar, and is now perched awaiting to be approached! Well, it won't be me, she decided.

Sure enough, Patrick Davies was approached and entered into dialogue with a young lady with curly blonde hair, large blue eyes, and enthusiastic arm movements. The young blonde brought him to Hannah, who gave him a welcoming hug and kiss. "Patrick! I'm so glad you came" and she proceeded to introduce him to the rest of the networking flock.

"Pammi, have you met Patrick?" Hannah asked Pamela. "No, I haven't. Hi Patrick." "Patrick designs websites. He is the go-to guy for your online branding and presence. I'm telling you, his roster includes really big names in the music industry and even restaurants and a casino in Johannesburg!". "Oh wow," said Pamela, not impressed. "You two would work perfectly together. Patrick, with your clever online marketing and Pamela with her vast PR contacts and media, know-how. A match made in heaven. P-Squared!" They all laughed.

Fast forward to three years later on August 28th when Hannah, Pamela and Patrick are on the beach in Grace Bay, Turks and Caicos. Hannah in a royal blue satin ruched bridesmaid's dress with a champagne glass in her hand. Patrick in a light Grey classic Saville Row three-piece with a royal blue tie and a baby blue rose head in his right lapel. He held a champagne glass in his left hand, which was now adorned with a platinum Cartier wedding band. And Pamela looked mesmerising in an exquisite white mermaid appliqué wedding dress with a sweep train. She was holding a bouquet of roses, all different tones of blue in her right hand, and holding out her left hand to show Hannah her five-line diamond wedding band. The wedding band was inscribed 'Mrs Davies'.

Hannah held her champagne glass high and toasted to the new couple, "Cheers to P-Squared! A match made in heaven".

CHAPTER FOUR

P-Squared

The match made in heaven lasted a while. But it had now been eight years and the heaven had become a little hellish. The whole P-Squared thing worked perfectly for the duo as neither Pamela nor Patrick liked keeping company with others unless required. Christmas, Birthday Parties, Weddings, and Business Events they would make an effort and moan in unison as they got ready. But seeing the reflection of how well turned out they looked side by side in their hallway mirror, brought some excitement and pride in the fact they were the handsome and beautiful Mr and Mrs Davies. Together they would step out and steal the limelight and what a rush it was to be 'couple goals' hashtag P-Squared!

By year eight of the marriage, they no longer moaned and grumbled in unison. Patrick used business meetings and working late and office commitments to not RSVP. Hashtag P-Squared stopped trending not only for public events but also privately in their home and business. Pacific Rose was named after Patrick's dad and Pamela's Mum. It was a partnership with an equal workload, equal power, and equal reward. But somehow Patrick had managed to push Pamela away from Pacific Rose.

Indeed, Pamela never enjoyed having to go to the office, especially in winter, waking up in the dark and returning home in the dark. Having to fake a smile and play office politics and watch females flirt with your husband all day was exhausting at best and depressing at worst. She decided she would work from home twice a week which became three times a week and then that became only when an important client was attending. Patrick tried his best to motivate her to get up at 6 am with him and get ready but she couldn't be bothered, especially as her role became more and more one of oversight and signing off. So he gave up and she had a replica executive office built at home with video conferencing capabilities. Happy wife happy life!

But no. Pamela was not happy. Her absence from the office left her out, she wasn't in sync with day to day occurrences and became very frustrated. She decided she would start attending the office again but she felt unwelcome, less respected, and unsupported or empowered by her husband. She was angry with herself for becoming so complacent, that she had lost her power and presence in the company. Pacific Rose was also her baby but now she had nothing to do with it. The more frustrated she got sat at home in her useless executive office the more Prosecco she drank. And no one cared, no one noticed, the success train carried on without her. She was replaceable like any of the other employees, replaceable like those executive assistants.

Pamela had enough, she procured a gym at home and began to punch punching bags instead of popping Prosecco corks. She became reinvigorated and alert. She slowly got her PR friendship circle back and began organising events. She loved it. She could be a hermit planning away and then socialise with everyone at once, in one big bang. Her enterprise was a success, she raised money for good causes and was once again happy. But in gaining her happiness she had lost her husband. He hated events, social networking, small talk. So he didn't support his wife as best he could. And now with full reign of Pacific Rose, he was much happier sitting as the big wolf in the office than attending galas with the Mrs.

P-Squared grew apart. Rumours of affairs were bad enough but then came the bombshell... rumour of an illegitimate son! "How dare he!" Pamela yelled repeatedly through the house when the unsolicited email from a former executive assistant came through. The email provided intimate details about Patrick, birthmarks, tattoos, scars, warts, and all. Pamela felt like she was boiling inside as she read the email, her heartbeat was so strong it shook the computer monitor. She wanted to cry but no tears would come to alleviate her stress. Her stomach was in knots as she read on. 'I hope you don't mind me approaching you, but it's only fair that Patrick's son is acknowledged'. Pamela responded with 'noted.'

Pamela screamed in anger as she tore herself away from the screen, she stormed into their dressing room to find her bag and car keys. She glimpsed her reflection in the large mirror that used to reflect 'couple goals'. Today it reflected rage, pain, and anger. She took a shoe from the shelf and threw it at the mirror. The heel that spelt YSL hit the mirror and it cracked from side to side. Now the tears came, strong and heavy like a rapid.

Patrick had kept delaying them from starting a family because of the needs of the business but here he was with his own child. She drove to the Pacific Rose headquarters and caused hell! Patrick had denied all of it but his pleas of innocence fell on deaf ears. She embarrassed him in his realm, he is the big bully in this playground and here she was shredding him to pieces in front of his subjects! How dare she make him inferior!

CHAPTER FIVE

Perfect wasn't Enough

It turned out the baby was not Patrick's.

But the damage had been done. Patrick resented Pamela for the nightmare he had to endure in clearing his name, he resented her because he had tried to motivate her and be her rock but she had forgotten. She had forgotten that it was him that would rush home in the middle of the day when she missed client conference calls and find her drunk and slumped in her black leather and walnut executive armchair. It was him that carried her to the shower to wake her up, dried her off, and put her to bed. He came home every night with flowers, chocolates, tickets to the theatre and kisses...lots of cuddles and kisses. He constantly reminded her of her beauty and how he adored every curve of her body. He was a loving husband, who only ever wanted it to be just the two of them, but that wasn't enough for her. She needed the praise of others and constant opportunities for her virtue signalling. He had been the perfect husband but perfect wasn't enough.

Pamela didn't care that the baby was not Patrick's. She resented him for being unfaithful, she resented that she was not enough for him and that he needed a string of executive assistants. But she couldn't divorce him, she would lose too much. She would be left with just a house and her events. There were no children, so the parting of ways would be simple, with no ongoing support. No, she wasn't going anywhere, not for now.

She needed to plan this properly, execute it well, and then move on. She was still young, still beautiful, and well connected. She began plotting her way out with more than just a house. It wasn't fair that she would get meagre portions when she had been so accommodating to Patrick and his ego. It was she that he would practise speeches in front of and she would correct him, clap for him and reassure him. She provided valuable input into campaigns for female clients with her woman's point of view. She hugged him and kissed him and told him how handsome he was every time he left for work. She kept her body in shape so that he could show off his trophy wife with the brains when collecting his business awards. She wiped his tears when his father died and took on the office, the house, and the funeral preparations as he was too devastated to manage things.

    She had been the only constant female in his life apart from his grandmother and unlike his mother, who ran away with one of his father's music artists, she had remained faithful. Pamela had been the perfect wife, but perfect wasn't enough for Mr Davies.

CHAPTER SIX

March 28th

It was March 28th and Pamela Davies was busy! She had a big gala planned for April 02nd and became more hysterical as the date grew nearer. The house was buzzing with deliveries, builders, gardeners, and people! Lots of people. Despite the very large size of her home, it had never been used by so many inhabitants. Pamela Davis, though well known and respected, preferred her own company. Guests would rarely come to the house, instead, she would utilise Vincenzo at the office to arrange lunch at The Palm Beach or dinner at the Pearson Rooms but never the home address. This is why this gala was even more important because it was showcasing her home, and providing a glimpse into her otherwise private life.

Security systems were being maintenance checked, alarms set off, motion cameras tricked into action. All the notifications and alerts were sending Pamela's gold plated, large-screen iPhone into a frenzy. Parts of the garden that Pamela didn't bother with, now needed to be considered. Flowers were planted, weeds were removed, old garden ornaments were thrown away and new garden swing beds and fire pits were being installed. Winter had been bitter and lasted into late March, the wind was still crisp, sharp and chilly. But Pamela's guests were promised a cigar and shisha terrace and so this would be catered for.

"We will need blankets on these outdoor couches," said Pamela as she pointed out the outdoor seating arrangements to her event planner, Kim.

"Of course Mrs Davies" replied Kim.

"It's a shame that it's still so cold! It better not rain, no one comes out in the rain. Mother Nature darling, April showers will need to hold out till after my gala". They laughed.

"We've checked again today and the probability of rain is low and if there is any it will clear by 2 pm. Which is fine as we start at 8 pm" Kim said reassuringly.

The two women laughed, pointed, and talked as they walked into the large entertaining room which was set up to host forty guests with five per table. Candle Lit chandeliers hung above each table. The tables were round with a revolving marble centre. They each had large fuschia coloured orchids submerged into water-filled, glass vases as the centrepiece. Pamela reviewed the rose head adorned nameplates, with a keen interest in where she was positioned and specifically who was sat in her group of five. To her left, the nameplate read "James T. Georgestone". James was a property tycoon with a liking for fast cars, island getaways, and beautiful women. To her right was "Christopher Appiah" also known as Big Chris. Christopher was from old money, he had generational wealth which he wasted on cigars, gluttonous meals, and divorce settlements. The woman placed to his right was the current Mrs Appiah, wife number four.

"I wanted to confirm that this is correct, and you were quite sure you didn't require Mr Davies to be placed on this table." Asked Kim.

"Kim, when has Patrick ever arrived on time to my events and that's if he arrives at all? I am not sitting next to an empty seat in my own house!"

Pamela was right. Mr Davies never attended her soirées and when he did he made a guest appearance and found an excuse to leave early, or he arrived just before the end to take the mandatory wife and husband photo for the media outlets. Mr Davies did not like these events, partly because like his wife he was happier in his own company and partly because he would not be the most powerful man in the room. He ruled the office, he ruled his business realm, he ruled his home but outside of arenas in which he ruled he was quite insecure. He knew a lot about digital media and big data, but who wants to sit at dinner and talk about that for two hours.

Patrick wasn't very charismatic and got away in social situations by using his good looks, his style, his swagger, his athletic silhouette, and his aura of power. In a room full of powerful, rich men, Patrick felt that good looks and style were second place. He didn't like anything other than first place. So his ego and insecurities would not allow him to attend his wife's events, not at least until the dinner and conversation part was over with. Dancing and taking photos and short greetings while edging towards the exit, he could do.

CHAPTER SEVEN

The Business Trip

"Fountayne!" Yelled Mr Davies from the doorway of his executive office at Pacific Rose H.Q.

Ella, who was swiping through shoe options on her red python leather-backed iPhone with the girls from finance, got up from her desk and walked into Mr Davies' office. The office was a considerable size with a floor to ceiling glass sliding door that let in a lot of light from the south-facing terrace. The terrace was situated to the right of Mr Davies' desk and had large potted green plants in black ceramic vases. There was an oak wooden bench on the terrace that was frequently used by clients such as Big Chris, who would smoke his cigar as he detailed his requirements.

The terrace was overlooked by the 'Icon Peninsula', a newly built hotel that housed both guests and residents. It was currently the city's most expensive apartment block.

Inside, the office was decorated in muted earthy tones. The wall panels were upholstered in a bluish-grey flannel. The large rectangular desk was walnut with a black leather writing area. The desk stood on a luxury rug of the same blueish grey tones as the wall. To the left of the desk were bespoke custom-built walnut bookshelves that showcased awards, miniature cars, and a few books. A chandelier of copper hung above the desk and armchair. The armchair was dark brown leather with a walnut frame. It mirrored the chair opposite the desk.

There was a smaller round oak table to the right of the terrace doors with four tan-coloured leather meeting room chairs that had chrome feet and black casters. Big Chris would frequently be seen spinning around in these chairs as he reviewed the outcome of his requirements.

"Take a seat." Mr Davies said as he pointed at the dark brown leather armchair opposite his. Ella obliged.

"The business travel for April 02nd, you'll have to go on your own. Pammi, my wife, has that thing she's doing and it won't be good if I don't make an appearance and show support for her little party. Especially as it's being held at the house."

"Sure," said Ella.

"I hope you're comfortable with that, I'll give you the proposal and clarify my motives so you'll know how to steer the agenda in our favour."

"Perfect, I'm comfortable with that" she assured him.

"As you'll be missing out on the flowing champagne and canapés of the gala, you can charter a jet. I'll have Vincenzo book that for you". He smiled at his gesture.

"Yes! I love it" she got up and walked out of the office "I expect champagne and canapés on the plane".

"Of course you do!" Laughed Patrick.

CHAPTER EIGHT

April 02nd

Mrs Davies wore a long black sequined dress that floated above the floor. Her toes were freshly pedicured with pastel pink nail polish. The diamanté straps of her heels could be seen as she glided into the gala. They were gasps as she walked in...the dress.

The sweetheart neckline of the dress enhanced her curvaceous figure and left her décolletage exposed and free to show off her white diamond necklace with the 10-carat canary yellow cushion diamond, that lay just above her bosom. Her hair was in a braided updo leaving the beauty of her heart-shaped face with upturned hazel eyes for all to see. Her lips were red. The lipstick colour was called 'Red Carpet' and how appropriate a name for this occasion.

Mrs Davies was in her element as she waltzed by each table. There were air kisses, hugs and 'darlings' galore. Her table was strategically placed so that it would be at the finish line of her welcome marathon. On arrival at her table, she greeted and hugged each of the guests and took her seat next to James and Christopher.

The revolving marble centrepiece was now filled with fruit and cheese and cuts of cold meat. Caprese garlic bread. Sweet chilli shrimp. Olives. Spicy pickled cucumbers. Seared halloumi on flatbread and small trays of oysters on shaved ice. Big Chris spun the centrepiece with glee!

It was 8.30 pm and the gala was off to a great start. The host was gracious and glamorous. The home was warm and inviting. The food was delicious and moreish.

CHAPTER NINE

The Bullet Trick

"Aren't you supposed to be at the gala?" asked Ella from the door of Mr Davies' office. She was wrapped up warm in a black Mackintosh, with a warm red scarf and black velvet gloves.

"Aren't you supposed to be at the airport?" came the response from Patrick. "You know It's not my thing, I'll make an appearance in the last hour. Anyway, can't you see I have to "work late today". He smiled as he took his glass of Hennessy on the rocks and sipped. He turned the volume down on the football he was watching and ushered Ella in.

Ella advanced into the office and a bright shiny object in Patrick's briefcase immediately caught her eye. It was a black and silver nine-millimetre Beretta nestled among a folded shirt, a passport, and a book 'The Bullet Trick' by Louise Welsh. The reflection of the silver gun glistened in her eyes and Patrick asked, "Does it interest you?"

She moved near his desk "Why do you have it?"

"It's for my wife". He said.

"Does she need protection?" Ella enquired.

"No, it's to get rid of her" He responded with a smile. Ella was not sure if he was being serious or weirdly sarcastic, she moved to the briefcase and picked up the gun.

"Put it down, it's not a plaything, and you have enough shiny items".

"Show me how it works?" She said.

"A beautiful lady never needs to know, you'll always have a strong man around to protect you." He laughed, then began to coach her on how to use the gun.

"There's nothing to it, you take the safety off right there. it's already loaded with bullets." Ella examined the gun.

"Stand firm, legs apart to handle the kickback". She took up the stance, legs firmly planted.

"Put your right hand on the top of the handle ready to pull the trigger and left hand on the bottom to steady your grip." She placed her hands as instructed.

"Then you just aim at your target and pull the trigger." She closed her left eye, aimed and Bang!

The bullet casing flew past Ella's right ear. The tip of the Beretta blew smoke into the air. The hollow-tipped bullet pierced into Patrick's heart and shattered. His head fell onto the leather writing pad of the walnut table, his white and blue striped fitted shirt streamed with bright cherry red blood.

The Rottweiler placed the gun back into Patrick's briefcase. She turned toward the door, picked up the bullet casing, pocketed it, and exited the now late Mr Davies' office.

CHAPTER TEN

Noted

Ella Fountayne took a seat on the private jet and placed her Chanel bag on the seat next to her. She sipped on a glass of champagne as the staff busied around her, bringing out canapés and placing her bags into the overhead lockers. Ella was handed a small warm towel by the air hostess, she wiped her hands and then reached into the inside pocket of her Chanel bag. She took out a small black mobile phone and texted "flight take-off as planned, no delays."

Meanwhile, at the now heaving gala, the newly widowed Mrs Pamela Davies, took a small black mobile phone out of her Celine purse, read the message and responded.

As Ella Fountayne was about to turn the mobile phone to airplane mode, in came the response "Noted".

Printed in Great Britain
by Amazon